Goodnight Swogg
the Silly Frog

Grump C

Illustrated by:
Stefanie St.Denis

Tellwell Talent
www.tellwell.ca

ISBN
978-0-2288-2856-3 (Hardcover)
978-0-2288-2855-6 (Paperback)

Deep in Skunk Hollow, Swogg the Silly Frog lived most happily in a Bubbly Bog...

...with his ten best friends: Lucky Bucky Beaver, Eenie Meanie Earthworm, Glow the Rainbow Trout, Speedy

2

the Snail, Pinchy the Crayfish, Twinkles the Tadpole, Einstein the Blue Heron, Aunt Myrtle the Turtle, Crazy Cousin Cricket, and Mighty Minnow.

One night, Swogg was very tired
but he could not get to sleep...

KNEEDEEEP

CHIRRUP CROOOAK

RIBBIIITT

CRRRICKET

...because -- the Bubbly
Bog was TOOOO LOUD!

Swogg thought and thought.
What shall I do?

Shall I swim over and tell the other frogs and crickets to be QUIET?

7

OR cover my ears and try to ignore all the loud noises?

8

And that is exactly what Swogg the Silly Frog did -- he fell asleep! Goodnight, Swogg.

Grump C's ODE to Grandpa Carl

Swogg the Silly Frog was inspired by my favorite person, Grandpa Carl, who was born almost 120 years ago in 1901. Carl spent almost every afternoon for over 40 years dreaming, creating, searching, building, relaxing, and enjoying his heavenly hideaway -- Skunk Hollow.

Located in central Wisconsin, Skunk Hollow has a beautiful wooden cabin and a gorgeous pond fed by natural springs from two bubbling brooks. Carl shared his hideaway Skunk Hollow with only his best friends and family.

I was able to spend more than 30 of my best years with Grandpa Carl at Skunk Hollow. Appreciating nature, becoming worry-free, and especially enjoying zany experiences with family and friends make Skunk Hollow absolutely my favorite place. Now a proud grandfather just like Grandpa Carl, I am thrilled Hadley, Tommy, and Ella have joined our funny family. It is my passion to share Grandpa Carl's hideaway and Swogg the Silly Frog's creativity and zany antics with all of you.

CPSIA information can be obtained
at www.ICGtesting.com
Printed in the USA
LVHW070017131020
668649LV00015B/480